THE WAY WE DO IT IN JAPAN

written by GENEVA COBB IIJIMA

illustrated by PAIGE BILLIN-FRYE

ALBERT WHITMAN & COMPANY

MORTON GROVE, ILLINOIS

To my grandsons, Jonathan Toshiro and John Paul. With special appreciation to my son, Timothy, whose childhood experience in Japan prompted the writing of this story. — G. C. I.

To my kids, Marty and Tony. — P. B-F.

I wish to thank those who aided me in the preparation of my book: My daughter, Crystal, who gave me excellent critiques on my manuscript; Katie Cole, Mihoko Ami, and my son Stephen's wife, Christine, for providing their insights about life in Japan; and Theresa Dion, who gave me artistic advice. — G. C. I.

Many thanks to Junko Sato; Brenda Seat; Caoilfhionn O'Drudy, from the Japanese Information and Cultural Center in Washington, D.C.; and Bob Evans, from the Capital Children's Museum in Washington, D.C. — P. B-F.

Library of Congress Cataloging-in-Publication Data
Iijima, Geneva Cobb.
The way we do it in Japan / by Geneva Cobb Iijima ; illustrated by Paige Billin-Frye
p. cm.

Summary: Gregory experiences a new way of life when he moves to Japan with his American mother and his Japanese father.
ISBN 0-8075-7822-3 (hardcover)
[1. Japan—Fiction.] I. Billin-Frye, Paige, ill. II. Title. PZ7.1275 Way 2002 [E]—dc21
2001004091

The illustrations are rendered in watercolor, gouache, acrylic, and colored pencil.
The design is by Scott Piehl.

For more information about Albert Whitman & Company,
visit our web site at www.albertwhitman.com.

T HIS STORY IS ABOUT GREGORY, whose mother, Jane, came from Kansas and whose father, Hidiaki,* came from Japan. They all lived together in a little house in San Francisco until …

* Hee-dee-ah-kee

Gregory's dad returned from work one day with big news!

"My company is sending me to Japan," he announced to Gregory and his mom.

"I want to go, too!" said Gregory.

"We'll all go," said Mom. "We will live like Japanese and eat with chopsticks."

"Why?" asked Gregory. "I like forks better."

"Because," said Mom, "that's the way we'll do it in Japan."

Soon Mom and Dad began packing up the dishes, sheets, and towels, and Gregory packed his toys and clothes. He wondered what kind of toys Japanese children played with, and what kind of clothes they wore.

At the airport Gregory hurried to the plane, ready for the long flight.

"Ohayoo gozaimasu," * said the stewardess.

"What did she say?" asked Gregory.

"She said 'Good morning,'" replied Dad.

"Ohayoo gozaimasu," Gregory called after her.

oh-ha-yoh goh-zah-ee-mah-suh

The stewardess brought him rice and fish for lunch.
Gregory wrinkled his nose. "I don't like fish," he whispered
to Mom. But he ate all the rice and a little of the fish.
He was glad he knew how to use the chopsticks on his tray.

"This is the way they eat in Japan," he told the girl across
the aisle. She was eating with a fork.

After they arrived at the airport near Tokyo, Gregory's dad went to the bank to exchange his American money for some Japanese money.

"May I have a dollar?" asked Gregory.

"How about a 100 yen piece?" his dad said.

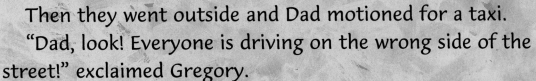

Then they went outside and Dad motioned for a taxi.

"Dad, look! Everyone is driving on the wrong side of the street!" exclaimed Gregory.

His dad laughed. "That's not the wrong side. That's the left side. That's the way we do it in Japan."

They drove along an expressway until they arrived on the edge of Tokyo and stopped at a tall apartment building. When Gregory's dad paid the fare, the taxi driver said, "Domo arigatoo."*
And Gregory knew that he had said thank you.
"Do itashimashite,"** replied his dad.

*doh-moh ah-ri-gah-toh
**(you're welcome): doh ee-tahsh-ee-ma-she-te

The apartment manager showed them to the fifth floor. He opened the door and gave them the key.

Gregory's dad took off his shoes in the entryway and left them on the tile floor. "The Japanese like to keep their floors very clean," he said. "So you wear your slippers inside the house."

Gregory glanced at the floppy slippers, but he just kicked off his shoes and ran into the apartment to look around. Instead of carpet, like in his house in San Francisco, the living room floor was made of tightly woven straw.

He looked at Dad.

"That's the—" began Dad.

"I know," interrupted Gregory. "That's the way we do it in Japan."

"But aren't there any chairs in the living room?" Gregory asked.

Dad pointed to some pillows around a low table. "Those are zabuton,"* he said. "They're to sit or kneel on while eating or visiting."

*zah-boo-tohn

"I'm tired," Mom said, sighing. "It's been a long day.
Let's get ready for bed."

Gregory looked around. "How will we sleep?" he asked.
"There are no beds in this apartment."

Dad laughed. He opened the closet. "These are the beds," he said, as he pulled out colorful mattresses. "People here sleep on the floor."

"Wow! That'll be just like camping!" Gregory said excitedly.

Gregory went to take a bath. The tub looked so strange!
It was square and deep, and the shower was on the outside
of the tub.

"The shower is to wash yourself off before you take your
bath," explained Dad. "Japanese sit with their knees up and
just relax in the hot water while they're in the tub."

Gregory took off his clothes and washed off under the
shower.

When he was clean, he dipped his toe into the water in
the tub. It was hot, but he slowly eased himself into it.
After his long day, the water felt good.

"I like the way we do it in Japan," he said.

In the morning Gregory and his dad went shopping for school supplies.

"Those book bags look huge," said Gregory. "And don't you have any blue ones?"

"The girls all wear red ones, and the boys wear black ones. That's the custom," the clerk told them. "But at your school the students wear blue gym uniforms on days they have gym. And you'll need a red cap, too."

Gregory tried on the hat. "It looks nice," he said.

The next day Gregory felt proud walking along under the cherry trees beside his father and carrying his book bag on his back. Inside were his new notebook and pencils and his red hat. He carried his lunch bag from San Francisco with his favorite superhero on it.

As they neared the school, he felt a little scared, though. *Will the kids like me?* he wondered.

When they arrived at school, the principal spoke to him in English. "Welcome to South Tokyo Elementary School. I hope you are very happy."

"Thank you," said Gregory softly. Then he blinked back a tear as he said good-bye to his father and followed the principal to his classroom.

"Your teacher, Inoue-sensei,* speaks English. You will do fine," the principal said.

*(Inoue — teacher's name): *Ee-noh-oo-ey*

*(sensei — teacher): *sen-say*

Inoue-sensei showed him to a desk and handed him a mathematics book. Gregory looked through the book. The numbers were written the same as in America, but he knew they were pronounced differently. His father had already taught him that. In his mind Gregory counted to five in Japanese: ichi, ni, san, shi, go.*

*(one, two, three, four, five): *ee-chee, nee, sahn, shee, goh*

But when reading class began, he felt very alone. How would he ever learn to read those funny marks?

While the other children studied their reading books, Inoue-sensei showed Gregory how to write the letters in the Japanese alphabet. He worked hard and was very glad when lunchtime came

That is, until the children who were kitchen helpers brought in trays of rice, fish, and fermented soybeans.

Gregory looked at his own lunch—a peanut butter sandwich, an apple, and cookies. He had the wrong kind of lunch!

Out of the corner of his eye, he saw the other students watching him as he ate. His face flushed, and he had a hard time swallowing.

When the teacher dismissed them for recess, the boy in the seat across from him said, "I, Yuuki,"* and motioned for him to follow.

On the playground they played soccer. Gregory liked soccer. Yuuki saw that he could play well and smiled.

Yoo-oo-kee

When the bell rang, Yuuki put on his red cap and grabbed a cloth and some window cleaner. He gave Gregory a cloth, too. Then he began washing the classroom windows. Gregory looked around. Other children were sweeping the floor or dusting. *This is the way we do it in Japan,* he thought. It even looked kind of fun.

When the room was clean, they returned to their desks for geography class.

When he got home Gregory knelt beside the table and practiced writing the Japanese alphabet all evening.

The next morning he wore his new gym uniform, and he left his lunch bag home.

Mom helped him put his book bag on his back and kissed him good-bye.

Gregory smiled as he walked to school. Today he felt almost like a real Japanese schoolboy.

Near school some older boys pointed at him and he heard them say, "Amerikajin."*

Gregory sighed. He wondered if he ever would fit in.

*(American): *Ah-meh-ree-ka-jeen*

Then he saw Yuuki running toward him. Yuuki began talking excitedly in Japanese. Gregory laughed. Even if he didn't understand what Yuuki said, it was good to have a friend.

Gregory gave Inoue-sensei his homework when it was time for handwriting class.

"Very good," she said. "You are learning quickly."

When Inoue-sensei announced lunch, the kitchen helpers came in with a big bowl of rice and a tray of fish. Gregory looked down at his desk and bit his lip. *I don't want rice and fish*, he thought.

Suddenly, he heard all the children cheering happily. When he looked up, children were bringing in tray after tray of peanut butter and jelly sandwiches!

Gregory was confused. He pointed to the rice and fish. "But that's the way we do it in Japan," he said.

"And this is the way you do it in America," said Inoue-sensei, smiling.

"Amerikawa sugoi!"* shouted the children.

*(America is wonderful): *Ah-meh-ree-ka-wa su-go-ee*

THE SUN PLAYS an important part in the ancient mythology of Japan, and for centuries Japanese people have called their country "Land of the Rising Sun." Their flag even has a big red sun on it.

Four main islands and hundreds of smaller ones make up the country of Japan. On Hokkaido, the northern island, the winters are long and very cold. Summers are hot on Kyushu, the southern island. The central islands, Shikoku and Honshu, have moderate temperatures throughout the year. All four islands together are about the size of California.

When people are first introduced to each other in Japan, they bow instead of shaking hands. Bows are also exchanged between friends when they meet on the street or visit each other.

A typical Japanese meal is made up of soup, rice, fish or meat, and pickled vegetables. Noodles are also popular, served hot or cold in broth. Many foods are made with soybeans, including *tofu* (soybean curd) and *miso*, a paste used to make a flavorful soup.

Japanese children have their own special holidays. On March 3, Girls' Day (also known as Doll Day), girls dress up in kimonos, visit friends and family, and display a special set of dolls. Boys' Day is May 5. On this day, families celebrate the health and happiness of children, and households with sons hang out carp-shaped streamers called *koi-nobori*. Carp represent strength and courage, traits parents hope their sons will develop.

In Japan, the school year starts in April and goes until the following March. On Saturdays children go to school for half a day, and many students stay in the afternoon to take part in club activities or practice sports such as baseball or soccer.

There are three kinds of writing in the Japanese language. Children in primary school learn to read and write using the *Katakana* and *Hiragana* alphabets, which have fifty-one letters each. As children grow older, they learn to read and write the more complex writing system using Chinese characters known as *Kanji*. There are thousands of Kanji characters, and people continue to learn them all their lives.

Japanese children study English from about the fourth grade. They are often eager to learn about America and the way Americans live. As friends, Americans and Japanese have much to discover from each other.

JP
Iijima, Geneva Cobb.
The way we do it in Japan /

05/09/11